THIS BOOK BELONGS TO :

Made in United States
Troutdale, OR
12/14/2023

15812975R00031